MR. STRONG

by Roger Hargreaves

EGMONT

This is the story of Mr Strong.

Mr Strong is the strongest person in the whole wide world.

The strongest person there has ever been, and probably the strongest person there ever will be.

He is so strong he can not only bend an iron bar with his bare hands, he can tie knots in it!

Mr Strong is so strong he can throw a cannonball as far as you or I can throw a tennis ball!

Mr Strong is so strong he can hammer nails into a wall just by tapping them with his finger.

Strong by name and strong by nature!

And would you like to know the secret of Mr Strong's strength?

Eggs!

The more eggs Mr Strong eats, the stronger he becomes.

Stronger and stronger and stronger!

Anyway, this story is about a funny thing that happened to Mr Strong one day.

That morning he was having breakfast.

And for breakfast he was having … eggs!

Followed by eggs. And to finish, he was having – guess what?

That's right. Eggs!

That was Mr Strong's normal breakfast.

After his eggy breakfast, Mr Strong cleaned his teeth.

And, as usual, he squeezed all the toothpaste out of the tube.

And, as usual, he cleaned his teeth so hard he broke his toothbrush.

Mr Strong gets through a lot of toothpaste and toothbrushes!

After that he decided to take a walk.

He put on his hat and opened the front door of his house. CRASH!

"What a beautiful day," he thought to himself and, stepping outside his house, he shut his front door.

BANG! The door fell off its hinges.

Mr Strong gets through a lot of front doors!

Then Mr Strong went for his walk.

He walked through the woods.

But, he wasn't looking where he was going, and walked slap bang into a huge tree. CRACK!

The huge tree trunk snapped and the tree thundered to the ground.

"Whoops!" said Mr Strong.

He walked into town.

And again, not looking where he was going, he walked slap bang straight into a bus.

Now, as you know, if you or I were to walk into a bus, we'd get run over.

Wouldn't we?

Not Mr Strong!

The bus stopped as if it had run into a brick wall.

"Whoops!" said Mr Strong.

Eventually, Mr Strong walked through the town and out into the country. To a farm. The farmer met him in the road, looking very worried.

"What's the matter?" asked Mr Strong.

"It's my cornfield," replied the farmer. "It's on fire and I can't put it out!"

Mr Strong looked over the hedge, and sure enough the cornfield was blazing fiercely.

"Water," said Mr Strong. "We must get water to put out the fire!"

"But I don't have enough water to put a whole field out," cried the worried farmer, "and the nearest water is down at the river and I don't have a pump!"

"Then we'll have to find something to carry the water," replied Mr Strong.

"Is that your barn?" he asked the farmer, pointing to a barn in another field.

"Yes, I was going to put my corn in it," said the farmer. "But …"

"Can I use it?" asked Mr Strong.

"Yes, but …" replied the perplexed farmer.

Mr Strong walked over to the barn, and then do you know what he did?

He picked it up. He actually picked up the barn!

The farmer couldn't believe his eyes.

Then Mr Strong carried the barn, above his head, down to the river.

Then he turned the barn upside down.

Then he lowered it into the river so that it filled up with water.

Then, and this shows how strong Mr Strong is, he picked it up and carried it back to the blazing cornfield.

Mr Strong emptied the upside down barn full of water over the flames

Sizzle. Sizzle. Splutter. Splutter.

One minute the flames were leaping high into the air. The next minute they'd gone.

"However can I thank you?" the farmer asked Mr Strong.

"Oh, it was nothing," remarked Mr Strong modestly.

"But I must find some way to reward you," said the farmer.

"Well," said Mr Strong, "you're a farmer, so you must keep chickens."

"Yes, lots," said the farmer.

"And chickens lay eggs," went on Mr Strong, "and I rather like eggs!"

"Then you shall have as many eggs as you can carry," said the farmer, and took Mr Strong over to the farmyard.

Mr Strong said goodbye to the farmer, and thanked him for the eggs, and the farmer thanked him for helping.

Then Mr Strong, just using one finger, picked up the eggs, and went home.

Mr Strong put the eggs carefully down on his kitchen table and went to close the kitchen door.

CRASH! The door fell off its hinges.

"Whoops!" said Mr Strong, and sat down.

CRUNCH! The chair fell to bits.

"Whoops!" said Mr Strong, and started cooking his lunch. And for lunch he was starting with eggs. Followed by an egg or two. And then eggs. And then for his pudding he was having …

Well, can you guess? If you can, there's no need to turn this page over to find out that he was having …

… ice cream!

Ha! Ha!

Fantastic offers for Mr. Men fans!

**Collect all your
Mr. Men or Little Miss books in
these superb durable collector's cases!**

Only £5.99 inc. postage and packaging, these wipe
clean, hard wearing cases will give all your Mr. Men
and Little Miss books a beautiful new home!

MR. NOBODY

Everybody's a Somebody

STICK £1
COIN HERE
(For poster only)

**Keep track of your favourite
Mr. Men and Little Miss characters with this brilliant collector's
poster, now featuring Mr. Nobody!**

Collect 6 tokens and we will send you a giant-sized double-sided poster! Simply tape
a £1 coin in the space provided and fill out the form overleaf.

Only need a few Mr. Men or Little Miss to complete your set? You can order any of the titles on the back of the books from our Mr. Men order line on 0870 787 1724. The majority of orders are delivered in 5 to 7 working days.

TO BE COMPLETED BY AN ADULT

To apply for any of these great offers, ask an adult to complete the details below and send this whole page with the appropriate payment and tokens, to: MR. MEN CLASSIC OFFER PO BOX 715, HORSHAM RH12 5WG

☐ Please send me a giant-sized double-sided collector's poster.

AND ☐ I enclose 6 tokens and have taped a £1 coin to the other side of this page

---

☐ Please send me ☐ Mr. Men Library case(s) and/or ☐ Little Miss Library case(s) at £5.99 each inc P&P

☐ I enclose a cheque/postal order payable to Egmont UK Limited for £...................

OR ☐ Please debit my MasterCard / Visa / Maestro / Delta account (delete as appropriate) for £...................

Card no. ☐☐☐☐☐☐☐☐☐☐☐☐☐☐☐☐☐☐☐   Security code ☐☐☐

Issue no. (if available) ☐   Start Date ☐☐ / ☐☐ / ☐☐   Expiry Date ☐☐ / ☐☐ / ☐☐

Fan's name: ....   Date of birth: ....

Address: ....

....

Postcode: ....

Name of parent / guardian: ....

Email of parent / guardian: ....

Signature of parent / guardian ....

Offer is only available while stocks last. We reserve the right to change the terms of this offer at any time and we offer a 14 day money back guarantee. Please allow up to 28 days for delivery. This does not affect your statutory rights. Offers apply to UK only.
☐ We may occasionally wish to send you information about other Egmont books. If you would rather we didn't please tick this box.